and the
Lockdown

by **ANDREW STARK**   illustrated by **EMILY FAITH JOHNSON**

PICTURE WINDOW BOOKS
a capstone imprint

Published by Picture Window Books, an imprint of Capstone.
1710 Roe Crest Drive, North Mankato, Minnesota 56003
capstonepub.com

Library of Congress Cataloging-in-Publication Data
Names: Stark, Andrew (Ojibwa Indian), author. | Johnson, Emily Faith, illustrator. | Stark, Andrew (Ojibwa Indian). Liam Kingbird's kingdom. Title: Liam and the lockdown / by Andrew Stark ; illustrated by Emily Faith Johnson.
Description: North Mankato, Minnesota : Picture Window Books, an imprint of Capstone, [2024] | Series: Liam Kingbird's kingdom | Audience: Ages 5-7 | Audience: Grades K-1 | Summary: On a snowy day Liam's school is having a lockdown drill, but being shut in still makes eight-year-old Liam anxious--until he finds a errant caterpillar and focuses his attention on the chilled insect.
Identifiers: LCCN 2023020985 (print) | LCCN 2023020986 (ebook) | ISBN 9781484689035 (hardcover) | ISBN 9781484689028 (paperback) | ISBN 9781484689103 (pdf) | ISBN 9781484689141 (kindle edition) | ISBN 9781484689110 (epub)
Subjects: LCSH: Ojibwa Indians--Juvenile fiction. | Schools--Safety measures--Juvenile fiction. | Anxiety--Juvenile fiction. | Caterpillars--Juvenile fiction. | CYAC: Ojibwa Indians--Fiction. | Schools--Safety measures--Fiction. | Anxiety--Fiction. | Caterpillars--Fiction.
Classification: LCC PZ7.1.S73758 Lik 2023 (print) | LCC PZ7.1.S73758 (ebook) | DDC 813.6 [Fic]--dc23/eng/20230508
LC record available at https://lccn.loc.gov/2023020985
LC ebook record available at https://lccn.loc.gov/2023020986

Designer:
Tracy Davies

Design Elements:
Shutterstock: Daria Dyk, Oksancia, Rainer Lesniewski

Printed and bound in the USA. 5626

Table of Contents

MEET LIAM KINGBIRD!

Liam loves to draw!

Liam has a cleft lip.

Liam is Ojibwa.

Liam is a good thinker.

Liam speaks two languages.

Liam likes animals.

WHAT MAKES YOU SPECIAL?

Chapter 1

PRACTICE DRILL

Liam sat inside Mrs. Dakota's third-grade class. He watched snow fall outside a window. Morning recess had just ended. Liam's classmates talked as they waited for the next lesson.

Just then, a voice came out of

the classroom loudspeaker. Liam

did not hear what the voice said.

"Children!" Mrs. Dakota said.

Wham! The fancy new

classroom door slammed shut.

Then Liam heard the lock click.

His classmates got quiet.

"Students," Mrs. Dakota spoke softer this time. "Remember, this is just a drill."

Liam's face got hot. His heart beat hard like a drum. He wondered if others were nervous.

Liam watched Mrs. Dakota
move quickly through the
classroom. She double-checked
the door. She switched off the
lights. Then, she returned to the
front of the class.

"Buddy up, everyone!" Mrs.
Dakota said with a soft clap.
"Find your partner."

Each student had a partner
for these kinds of drills. Everyone
quickly paired up. Liam joined
his buddy on the other side of
the room.

"Hi, Oscar," Liam said, shyly.

Oscar shrugged. Liam's classmates called Oscar the "quiet kid." They sometimes called Liam that too.

Mrs. Dakota clapped again softly. "What do buddies do?" she asked the class.

"Stick together," Liam and others answered. "Never leave a buddy behind."

Mrs. Dakota waited for the students to quiet down again.

She held up three fingers on
her right hand. She pointed to
each finger as she said the letters
H, W, and E. "Can anyone tell us
what those letters mean?"

Together, the class replied,
"Hide, wait, evacuate."

Chapter 2

THE CATERPILLAR

Mrs. Dakota walked silently to
the front corner of the classroom.
Liam, Oscar, and the other
students followed.

She pointed at the small space
on the floor behind her desk.

"Everyone please be seated,"
Mrs. Dakota said.

Liam joined the other students
on the floor. They sat quietly.

As they waited, Liam started to worry. *When will this be over?* he wondered. *What is happening outside the door? What if I need to use the bathroom?*

Liam stared out the window. The playground was covered in snow. It looked almost invisible.

Then Liam spotted something
on the frosty windowsill—a
caterpillar. It was coiled up,
no bigger than a nickel. Liam
wondered how the fuzzy little
insect had gotten inside.

Liam reached toward the window. He felt the cold of the frosted glass. Liam carefully scooped the caterpillar into his hand.

"What are you doing?" Mrs. Dakota whispered.

Oscar and the other students stared at Liam.

"I found a caterpillar," Liam said, opening his hand. The caterpillar uncoiled itself. The other kids watched as its little legs started to move.

Chapter 3

BUDDY UP

"Whoa! What kind is it? Is it alive?" The other students shouted questions at Liam.

"Shhh!" Mrs. Dakota hushed her class. "Is it, Liam?" she asked softly. "Alive?"

Liam looked up at her, smiling.

Mrs. Dakota let everyone huddle closer to Liam as long as they stayed quiet. Then she reached onto her desk and grabbed a tissue box. She held it out to Liam.

Liam looked confused.

Mrs. Dakota pulled out the remaining tissues.

"For the caterpillar," she said. "Until you can find it a better home."

Liam lowered the caterpillar into the box.

"What do caterpillars eat?" asked a girl named Mika.

Liam shrugged.

"Lettuce," said a soft voice.

Liam turned and saw Oscar sitting next to him. "Caterpillars will eat lettuce," said Oscar. "We can get some at lunch."

"Cool!" a couple kids said.

"That's a great idea, Oscar," said Mrs. Dakota.

Liam and the others watched the caterpillar march around the inside of the tissue box. Liam's worried thoughts were gone. He barely noticed when the drill finally ended.

Mrs. Dakota stood and told the class to return to their desks.

Then she asked Liam, "What are you going to name it?"

Liam looked into the box and then over at Oscar. "Buddy," said Liam. "We're going to call him Buddy."

Oscar nodded at Liam and smiled.

FACTS ABOUT OJIBWA

WHAT'S IN A NAME?

The Ojibwa are Indigenous people also known as Ojibwe, Chippewa, Anishinaabe, and Salteaux, depending on where they live. Many live in southern Canada and in the northern Midwest and the northern Plains of the United States.

"BOOZHOO! HELLO!"

The Ojibwa speak an Algonquian language called Anishinaabemowin or Ojibwemowin, which are dialects that change slightly from region to region. Dialect includes word pronunciation, grammar, and vocabulary. Most speakers of Ojibwemowin live in parts of Michigan, Wisconsin, Minnesota, or southern Canada. A school in Wisconsin is called the Waadookodaading Ojibwe Language Immersion School. All of its classes are taught in the Ojibwa language.

A LONG, LONG TIME AGO . . .

The earliest Ojibwa stories were either handed down through oral histories or birch bark scrolls. These stories tell of the five original Ojibwa clans, or doodem. These were the Bullhead Fish (Wawaazisii), Crane (Baswenaazhi), Pintail Duck (Aan'aawenh), Bear (Nooke), and Little Moose (Moozoonsii). There was a sixth doodem, the Thunderbird (Animikii), but they were too powerful and had to return to the ocean.

WHAT'S FOR DINNER?

Today the Ojibwa live very much like many other Americans and Canadians and eat what they do. But the original Ojibwa people were hunters and gatherers. They survived on wild rice and corn, lots of fish, and small game like squirrels and rabbits.

OJIBWA KIDS: JUST LIKE YOU

In the past, Ojibwa kids played with handmade dolls and toys. Lacrosse was a popular sport among older children. Today Ojibwa kids go to school, play sports and video games, and hang out with their friends. However, many are still very connected to the outdoors and love to go hunting and fishing.

GLOSSARY

caterpillar (KAT-ur-pill-ur)—the long wormlike larva of a butterfly or moth

cleft lip (KLEFT LIP)—a condition in which the lip does not fully form before birth, resulting in a gap or opening in the lip; surgery can close the gap and may leave a small scar on the upper lip

drill (DRIL)—training or exercise

evacuate (ee-VA-kyoo-ate)—to remove or withdraw from an area

huddle (HUH-duhl)—to crowd together

invisible (in-VIZ-uh-buhl)—not able to be seen

nervous (NUR-vuhs)—worried or anxious

reservation (rez-ur-VAY-shun)—land reserved for Indigenous tribal nations; in the past, many Indigenous people were forcibly moved to reservations by the United States government

GIVE IT SOME THOUGHT

- Have you ever experienced a lockdown drill or a similar safety drill at school? How did it make you feel? Did you feel nervous or scared like Liam?

- Liam found a caterpillar during the drill and it brought him comfort. What are some things or objects that make you feel calm and reassured in difficult or unfamiliar situations?

- In the story, Liam and his classmates were instructed to buddy up during the lockdown drill. Why is it important to have a buddy or a partner at times like this? How does having a buddy make you feel safer?

- Oscar told Liam that caterpillars eat lettuce. Can you think of any other animals or insects that have specific foods that they like? How do animals find their food in nature?

ABOUT THE CREATORS

 Andrew Stark was raised on the Ojibwa Indian Reservation in Michigan's Upper Peninsula. After earning his MFA from Pacific University, he moved to Los Angeles and began his career as an editor for a fashion magazine. He has since been published in a variety of publications, and one of his short stories was adapted into a stage play. He lives in Saint Paul, Minnesota, with his two dogs—Gizmo, a Chihuahua, and Barney, a chiweenie. Together, they love to camp and go hiking.

 Emily Faith Johnson grew up on a farm in northern Wisconsin. She is a graphic designer, writer, and illustrator who loves bringing characters to life through her artwork. She's always secretly wanted to become a Broadway star, so when she's not writing or making art, you can usually find her serenading her goats and ponies with show tunes. She is a member of the Sault Ste. Marie Tribe of Chippewa Indians.